TUMBLING INTO AN ADVENTURE

ADVENTURE SERIES

BY

DR VEENA ADIGE

ISBN 978-93-5438-234-5

Published in India 2020 by Pencil

A brand of
One Point Six Technologies Pvt. Ltd.
123, Building J2, Shram Seva Premises,
Wadala Truck Terminal, Wadala (E)
Mumbai 400037, Maharashtra, INDIA
E connect@thepencilapp.com
W www.thepencilapp.com

Author biography

Dr Veena Adige is a journalist who worked as Asst Editor of an English newspaper and later as Associate Editor of a fortnightly English magazine. She currently freelances for several magazines and newspapers. She is the author of five books and six ebooks.

She holds two Bachelor's degrees in Science and Mass Communications, two post graduate degrees in Public Administration and Linguistics and a Doctorate in Philosophy.

Deeply interested in women and children, she works with an English medium unaided school in a rural area near Mumbai, India, which caters to children of seven villages around. The school has 500 children, forty percent are girls . She was instrumental in starting Twinkle club for children in Nagpur which has 25,000 children as members She is a founder of Vsisters, an all women GSB group of Navi Mumbai. Dr Veena is currently the Jt Secretary of Bharatiya Vidya Bhavan' s Navi Mumbai Kendra.

She has written several articles on women and children and participated in discussions, programs relating to them and was on the panel of child adoption when she was in Nagpur. She researched extensively on social worker Baba Amte who gave home to leprosy affected people and physically challenged ones when leprosy was a dreaded disease and wrote a book on him for which the Ph.D degree was awarded in 2017 by the Zoroastrian College.

Dr Veena Adige's husband, formerly a top executive, is also now in the field of social work and the school management. Her children are well settled. Daughter lives in the USA and son lives in Mumbai with their families.

She recently addressed a session at the United Nations on March 12, 2018 during the CSW62(Commission for the Status of Women) fifteen day session through the Temple of Understanding, went as a delegate of the All India Behram Baugh Society(Zoroashtrian College). Topic: Challenges and opportunities faced by rural women and girls.

Contents

TUMBLING INTO AN ADVENTURE

Chapter 1

"We are off to Chikmagalur," sang Bunty lustily in the shower.

The other children in the building heard his voice loud and clear and were envious. They had all heard about Chikmagalur, a quaint little town atop the Western Ghats in Karnataka where Bunty and his sister Dimpi went year after year for their summer vacation. Their grandparents lived there in a large sprawling bungalow which had a lovely rose garden in front and a fruit orchard at the back. They also had three Alsatian dogs named Moti, Tiger and Dusty who followed Grandfather Pai everywhere, and five huge buffaloes who gave rich frothy milk every day.

'We are off to Chikmagalur' hummed Dimpi as she packed their bags with clothes, shoes, toys and games.

'Dimpi, you must look after Bunty and see that he behaves,' said Mummy coming with fresh laundered clothes in her arms. 'Also see that he obeys Granny and Grandpa and does not create any problems.'

'Yes, Mummy,' said Dimpi with a smile. She had been hearing all this for the last one month since they had decided to go to Chikmagalur by themselves. This was the first time they were going without their parents. Daddy had taken up a new project and Mummy could not get leave from her office. But they did not want to miss their annual trip and had promised that they would do everything that was told to them.

'And don't fight' continued Mummy. It was quite a long journey from Bombay to Chikmagalur and Grandpa would come to Kadur station to receive them. Kadur was twenty five miles from Chikmagalur. The railways did not go to Chikmagalur as it was on the mountain and visitors had to get down at Kadur and take a taxi or a bus to reach.

They adored their grandparents and knew that they were loved very much in return. They also knew that their grandparents were indulgent but, at the same time, they would stand no nonsense and would expect them to be good, honest and obedient. They were very disciplined and expected that all the children who came to their house were equally disciplined. The grandparents knew that when both parents were working, they tended to give in to the wishes of their children. But in Chikmagalur it was proper obedient behaviour and no nonsense.

'Why can't the clock go faster?" wondered Dimpi looking at it for the umpteenth time. She was looking forward to the journey as well since Mummy had packed a huge lunch for them consisting of all their favourites like jam roll, chutney sandwiches, besides sabji-roti , dahi-bhaath (for lunch), biscuits, chocolates and other things. They even had tetra packs of fruit drinks and a thermos flask of hot chocolate milk. Her mouth was watering at the thought of the sumptuous feast they would have on the train. The journey was worth the trouble also because of the feast it included.

Besides they would meet their cousins from Bangalore, Pune and Delhi. Suman was coming from Bangalore just a couple of days later while the others were reaching a week after.

'We will sing and dance, play and fight and have a merry time,' she thought happily.

At last it was time to go to the station.

'Don't get down at any station except Kadur,' warned Daddy 'And look after yourselves. Ring us as soon as you reach'.

'And behave yourselves,' added Mummy.

They nodded their heads and soon the train started. They were now entirely on their own and they hugged themselves in excitement.

'Faster than fairies, faster than witches, bridges and houses, hedges and ditches' they recited.

'This will be a different sort of a holiday,' declared Bunty,

'I feel it in my bones. I am sure we will have some adventure,' he continued little knowing how true it would be and that they would tumble headlong into an adventure which they would never forget in their lives.

They took great care during the journey and did not put out their hands from the windows or go to the entrance or get down at any station. They had promised their parents that they would not do all these things and they obeyed.

Long before Kadur came they were ready and waiting, their luggage packed neatly. They had thrown the used paper plates and napkins in the dustbin, tightly corked their bottles and closed the boxes carefully.

'Grandpa' they shouted jumping off the train as soon as it stopped. Kadur was a small station on the Western railway but quite a few people got down here. 'We are so very happy to see you. How are Granny and Moti and Dusty and Tiger?' they asked.

Grandpa smiled. Dear old Grandpa was just the same, fat and cheerful though he could be quite stern if necessary. He would not hesitate to give them a strong dressing down if they misbehaved or did not obey. Otherwise he was great fun.

'You have both grown up into nice, young people,' he said. Ramu the driver gave a cheerful grin and picked up their luggage.

Climbing into the car they began lapping up the rich green scenery all the twenty five miles to Chikmagalur. Everything, the trees, the roads, the fat jackfruits, the lakes, seemed to be welcoming them once more to their beloved place.

As Dandarmukhi Lake came into view they both fell silent, waiting for the first glimpse of Grandpa's house. It was a sight that was etched into their memories. The big house with its red tiled roof, the large gates opening wide to receive them and the red, yellow, pink and white roses nodding their heads in the gentle soothing breeze.

There it was, big and warm and cozy with Grandma waiting at the head of the small flight of stone steps. The three dogs came rushing as soon as Johnny, the servant opened the gates, wagging their tails and splitting their mouths in wide grins. The pink tongues were lolling waiting to lick the children and Grandpa. They rushed round them in excitement and jumped till Grandpa's 'Down' brought them to their feet and they quietened down.

'Bunty, Dimpi, how you have grown' said Grandma with a big smile on her pretty wrinkled face. 'In one year you have become almost grown up'.

When the hugging, questioning and the excitement had come down a bit, Granny said, 'Now wash your hands and feet and come into the kitchen'.

'Oh, Granny, wait,' said Dimpi, 'Let me have a quick look around.'

'Yes, she has to say hello to the roses, the lilies, the jasmines, the well, the buffaloes and...' grinned Bunty dodging a blow that Dimpi aimed at him.

He too wanted to go and look for their favourite spots, on top of the guava tree, behind the hay stack and other places.

Hand in hand the two children sped into the garden breathing the heavenly perfume of the flowers.

'Ummmm' said Dimpi dreamily, ' I miss all this in Bombay'. They peered into the well which was brimming with clear water as usual and went to the backyard to count the large jackfruits hugging the trees, the pears nestling among the leaves and the bright and lovely mangoes looking down on them.

The buffaloes were away to their grazing fields and would return only at dusk.

'How come the idlis are soft and heavenly here?' asked Bunty gulping down a dozen hot ones.

'The fresh air makes you hungry,' smiled Granny happily. She loved to have all the grandchildren around her. She had made lots of food and stored it for the summer when the hungry young ones would come.

That night as they got ready for bed after one of Granny's delicious dinners, Bunty repeated, 'I smell adventure this time. Oh what a lovely exciting feeling that is.'

'You read too many adventure stories, that is why you feel like that,' said Dimpi. 'I, on my part, am happy with just eating and relaxing and doing nothing. No school, no homework, just fun.' Said Dimpi.

'You will become like a fat cow if you don't exercise,' teased Bunty as he laid his head down to sleep. In two minutes flat he was asleep dreaming of adventure .

Chapter 2

Bunty and Dimpi awoke to the sounds of the farm. The cock was crowing early in the morning, the birds twittering and the buffaloes grunting which woke them up. At first they could not remember where they were. And then they both sprang up.

'We are at Chikmagalur', they said and rushed to brush their teeth. They went to find Granny already up and making a fine white rangoli at the entrance. Her deft fingers made a beautiful design within minutes.

'This is to welcome whoever comes here and to let them know that this is a happy and satisfied house,' she said straightening up from her task. She led them to the backyard where the buffaloes stood patiently waiting to be milked. She had a big spotless bucket in her hand and she squatted down near one of the animals and began milking her. The children never tired of watching her deft hands and the milk come frothing into the bucket.

'Granny, can I also milk the buffaloes?' asked Dimpi, 'I am very confident of doing it. I have watched you for so many years. Please Granny; I won't get this chance in Bombay'

Granny turned to her and considered, 'Dimpi, you are still too young. Next year, maybe,' she promised and Dimpi had to be satisfied with it. Granny gave them large glasses of fresh sweet milk to drink and then went for a quick bath.

Bunty looked at the buffaloes. They were huge and placid. Their soft black eyes were beautiful and even if they smelt a bit, it was a natural and earthy smell which was not available in Bombay. He felt tempted and thought he could easily ride them.

'What fun it will be if I can climb on a buffalo and ride her,' he thought mischievously, 'Dimpi cant do it and I will show her what I can do'.

'What are you going to do today?' asked Grandpa at breakfast. Bunty watched Moti, Tiger and Dusty following Grandpa into the dining room and waiting beside him waiting for tit-bits from his table. The dogs were like shadows of Grandpa. They never left him alone even for a single minute. When Grandpa was resting or reading, they would play with the children. But the minute Grandpa got up, they would rush to his side. It was nice to see Grandpa walking with his dogs in tow. Bunty imagined himself walking like that with soldiers beside him, ready to obey him implicitly.

'We will go and watch Johnny,' he said

Bunty and Dimpi went to the little field where Johnny was tending to the small vegetable patch. There were different vegetables growing. The soil was very fertile and they grew all that they needed. Only for rice and pulses they went to the weekly market otherwise they were quite self sufficient and self reliant. This kept them busy the whole day and also made them remain healthy.

'What would you like for lunch?' Johnny now asked, 'Fresh tomatoes and cucumber? Or sabji made of cauliflower?' Bunty and Dimpi enjoyed this part of the daily routine in Chikmagalur. One did not have to wait for the vegetable vendor or go to the market. Here all that one had to do was go into the vegetable patch and choose what one wanted for lunch or dinner. And it would be fresh and very tasty.

When it was summer vacation for them in Bombay, it was the beginning of the monsoon season in Chikmagalur. All the children helped Grandpa and Johnny sow the seeds and watched the shoots growing up. The tender fresh green shoots would soon mature into little plants which produced flowers or fruits or vegetables as per their nature.

'Coming here is like learning lessons in nature,' thought Dimpi happily. Here they were one with nature and spent most of their times outdoors, the soil firm beneath their naked feet, the fresh air playing with their hair. They would soon grow tanned and healthy, their skins glowing and bursting with health.

The day passed very quickly and it was time for the sun to say goodbye to people. The children felt their eyelids droop though it was still quite early. They had not watched the TV at all, they thought in wonder. Back home watching TV and fighting over the channels was their favourite evening sport. Here they had not even remembered it. Neither had they spoken to anyone over the phone. The phone was in Grandpa's study and rang only once in a while. They were far away from the artificial comforts of life. Their entertainment was the birds and the animals, the plants and the flowers, the sun and the air. For one month they would forget all the tensions of a fast life and relax totally, though they would be busy every minute of the day.

Two days later Suman, their cousin from Bangalore came with her father, their Uncle Vasudeva. She was Dimpi's age but looked smaller and thinner. She was an only child and a bit afraid of Bunty's fights. She was not used to the constant bickering between Bunty and Dimpi and was upset when they fought. But otherwise she too looked forward to their annual visits to Chikmagalur with the same excitement as they did.

'I want to ride Netravati today' announced Bunty suddenly after breakfast when they were alone. Netravati was the huge broad buffalo and they all liked her. Bunty had been thinking all night about this venture.

'Don't be silly,' said Dimpi, 'She wont allow you and anyway what will Granny say?'

'I wont tell Granny,' said Bunty obstinately, 'But I want to ride her.'

'You cant,' said Dimpi.

'Challenge?' questioned Bunty, a glint in his eyes. And Dimpi kept mulishly quiet thinking that Bunty would not have the courage to climb the big animal.

The three children went to the shed where the herdsman was collecting the animals for their daily routine grazing. Bunty climbed the low compound wall and waited. One by one the animals came out of the gate. Bunty looked at each of them carefully. He had to identify Netravati as she was, by far, the most placid of all, he knew. When Netravati passed, he took a flying leap and landed squarely on her broad back.

Dimpi and Suman held their breaths. What would happen now?

Netravati was scared and shocked. No one had ever sat on her back before. She was quite unused to the action. She turned and stared at Bunty for a moment. Stunned. Then she gave a big bellow and broke into a short run. She was too fat to run faster but she managed a short distance trying to dislodge Bunty from her back. She shook herself and snorted. She rushed this way and that, shaking all the time. All the other animals and people scattered, now knowing fully what was happening.

Bunty, now frightened, grabbed her large horns and hung to them for dear life. Netravati's back was slippery and he was finding it hard to steady himself.

The herdsman shouted trying to control the other animals that had also got panic stricken. There was quite a commotion and several passers-by collected to watch the fun and advise Bunty. Someone told him to slip off, someone advised him to the contrary. One fellow tried to grab the animal and steady her but had to run away as she showed no signs of stopping her move. It was a mad commotion with no one really knowing what to do. The herdsman, meanwhile was just shaking his head and he now sat down with a thud. Never had such a thing happened before and he did not know how to act.

Dimpi and Suman too shouted and all this brought Grandfather and Grandmother to the shed.

'What is all this?' Said Grandpa angrily, 'Bunty, what do you think you are doing? Get down at once.'

But Bunty couldn't. He tried but did not know what to do. He looked imploringly at Grandpa. Netravati was moving and he just did not have the courage to let go off her horns and slip down. He was now really very scared. He was getting bumped and he regretted ever having got on her back. What had made him jump on her, he wondered.

Dimpi and Suman started crying, wondering what would happen to poor Bunty.

'Stop her,' shouted the herdsman.

It took four hefty men to catch hold of Netravati and steady her. She was still stamping her feet and snorting. One man picked Bunty carefully from her back and put him down. His legs felt weak but he was satisfied that they did not give way and make him a butt of laughter and scorn. His act of defiance and bravery was not really that now, he felt miserable.

'I have a good mind to box your ears', said Grandpa angrily, 'You would have fallen off and broken your bones or you would have been trampled by the herd. Never do such things again'. Grandpa and Grandma were also very shaken.

'I am sorry, Grandpa;' said Bunty meekly.

Granny hugged him tightly and he could feel her shivering in fear. She then went to Netravati and pacified her with soothing words.

'She too is scared, you know,' said Granny softly, 'As much as you. She has never had such an experience before.'

'Whatever made you get on her?' continued Grandpa as they went inside the house. 'If I catch you doing such things again I will send you back to Bombay by the next train'. That was a threat which made Bunty decide not to indulge in such escapades again. His body was bruised and aching. Every movement made him groan. As Dimpi rubbed him with iodex that night she said, 'You deserve the pain. It was a stupid thing to do.'

'But what an adventure it was,' grinned Bunty 'And I fully enjoyed it'.

'Just because you did not fall off or get crushed' said Suman crushingly, 'If something had happened, if you had got a fracture or broken your head, you would have been in the hospital for many weeks and would have missed everything.'

Bunty continued grinning and took a pillow, held it by its ears and sat on it almost as if it was a buffalo. He knew that it was a wrong thing to do. And if something untoward had happened he would have had himself to blame. Now it was only his body that was aching. Every bone seemed to have got rattled in the experience and Bunty found it quite painful.

Chapter 3

'Let's go to Ratnagiri hill today,' said Dimpi the next morning. 'We generally go there at least once during our visits.'

Granny looked doubtful. Bunty and mischief went side by side. Naughtiness was second nature to him. Of course Dimpi and Suman were older and more sensible but the Netravati episode had made Granny really worried. These growing up children were more than a handful and she was responsible for their welfare during their visits especially when their parents were not there. Even Suman's father had gone on a tour leaving her at Chikmagalur.

Ratnagiri was a small hillock about an hour's walk from their house. The climb to the top took half an hour and the view was breathtaking. There was a little temple there which they visited every time they came to Chikmagalur. They were planning to go a little after lunch, the best time in this weather and have a picnic at the Ratnagiri summit, then come back by sundown.

Reluctantly Granny gave them her permission, packing them a hamper for the picnic. There were some sandwiches and stuffed parathas, some gulab jamuns, paper plates and napkins, some water and soft drinks. They wore sensible clothes and shoes and armed with the small hamper and water bottles set off for Ratnagiri.

The road to the hillock was lined with the bright red and yellow flowers that were rampant at this time of the year. Besides, there were large trees and fields along the way. A Polytechnic college was newly built and students flocked here during the term. Now it was silent and there was no hustle bustle or the chatter of young people.

They passed it and reached the foot of the hillock. They rested for some time as they were quite unused to so much walking. Back home their parents dropped them to school or the school bus carried them to school and brought them back.

'Isn't it so peaceful here?' questioned Suman, looking around her 'Time seems to stand still but it is never boring.'

'Or dull,' added Dimpi agreeing at once. 'I love being in Bombay but I love it equally well here also.'

'I love it more here' said Bunty always wanting to say things which could start an argument.

'That is because you don't like getting up early in the morning, going to school and studying. Here there is no one to scold you. Granny and Grandpa give you a long rope and you can get away with anything. Mummy and Daddy are stricter and would have thrashed you for the Netravati episode,' said Dimpi crushingly 'Thank your stars that nothing serious happened. I am going to report this to Daddy who will really scold you.'

'Don't you dare...'began Bunty, his shackles rising. But Suman quickly put in, 'We love school and so we like being in the city also but Chikmagalur is heavenly,' seeing an argument in the offing.

They resumed their walking and began climbing the hillock. It was Suman who felt a strange sensation long before the others experienced it. She turned and saw that this was caused by a hefty man stalking them. She had noticed him earlier but had not given him a second thought. Now he was nearing them and she pointed this to Bunty and Dimpi. He was dark but well built and had a tiny squint.

Before they could do or say something the man had come near and was asking, 'Are you the Pai grandchildren?'

They nodded and he looked very grim.

'I am sorry to tell you that your grandfather has just had a heart attack and he is asking for you three.' He said in a rush.

"What has happened?' asked Dimpi with a quiver in her voice.

'I don't know. I only know that your Granny has sent for a doctor and has asked me to bring you back home immediately.' The children were shocked. Grandpa had been quite hale and hearty when they had left an hour back. What had suddenly happened to him? How could he suddenly become so sick that Grandma had to rush for a doctor?

'Let's go home,' said Dimpi worriedly and began running down the hillock. Bunty and Suman followed her only to be summoned by the man, 'Wait' he said, 'It will take you an hour to walk back. I will take you in a taxi.'

The children hesitated. They had been told strictly that they should not accept lifts from strangers. It had been dinned into their heads from childhood. But then this fellow seemed to know their grandparents. He had known their names and had brought a message. Besides, hadn't he said that Granny had told him to bring them back? They were three of them and it was broad daylight, so they agreed even though they did not like his face which had bushy, handle bar moustaches and he spoke a peculiar version of the Hindi language. They internally felt they could not trust him but they had no option. Time was important. Grandma needed them and there was no time to lose. They had to reach home immediately.

At the foot of the hill the man summoned a cruising taxi and bundled them in the backseat, himself climbing in the front.

The children were too worried to say anything and kept quiet.

The taxi gathered speed and soon they were nearing their house. However, instead of slowing down they sped away.

'Stop, stop,' shouted the children,

'This is our house and you are going the wrong way.'

'I know' grinned the man jeeringly, 'I am taking you far, far away where no one will know you'.

They tried to open the doors of the car but were shocked to see that there were no handles. They couldn't open them. The glasses were also rolled up and there was no way to call out to passersby. Dimpi and Bunty banged on the windows but they were too fast for anyone to give them a second glance.

'This was only a ploy,' said Bunty angrily 'There is nothing wrong with Grandpa, you only wanted to kidnap us'.

'How smart you are,' said the man sarcastically.

The three of them tried to grab the driver and appeal to him. But, to their horror, they noticed the obvious -that the two were hand in glove with each other and now the driver was driving still faster. They shouted and kicked, they hit and pinched but to no avail. The men merely smiled and took no notice. The three children might have been just some flies for all that they cared. There seemed to be nothing that they could do except sit back and see what was going to happen and where they would be taken. Their hearts were beating so fast that they could almost hear the beats, their hands were chilly with fright and they were constantly telling themselves that they needed to have courage to face the situation and deal with it. They had no choice.

Now they were going away from the town and the number of people on the road had trickled down. The children were too frightened and did not know what to do. The girls began crying and sniffing.

'W-where are you taking us" asked Bunty at last. 'Grandpa must have informed the police by now and they will save us,'

'You will not be missed for another hour,' smirked the mustachioed man, 'That would be the time you would have taken to walk home. By then we will be far away'.

'Grandpa will find us,' said Dimpi tearfully but confidently. They were so frightened and worried that she felt she had to say something to keep their spirits up. They needed to think carefully about what to do now. The taxi was moving fast and going out of the town.

Now they were heading for the mountains, the greenery was thinning down and soon they turned off into a small bylane. This was bumpy and a rough road and in about fifteen minutes they reached a ramshackle house.

'Get out,' said the man who had kidnapped them, opening the door and shepherding them into the dirty dilapidated house. It was so dirty that they shuddered. It was obvious that this was an unused place. No one was living here and it must be a shady place for such people to carry on their dirty activities. How could they dare to bring three children here? Weren't they afraid of the consequences? Weren't they afraid of the police?

'Where are we?' asked Bunty, 'This seems to be the middle of nowhere. I am sure the police must be coming.'

'Ha-ha' laughed the man pushing them into a room and closing the door. They could hear the bolt slide into place. Suman almost fell down as the men were so very rough and Bunty got really mad at them. But they had gone away and no amount of banging on the door produced any result.

'What can we do?' said Suman fearfully. They looked around the dirty place. The room had just a bench in it, a small stool and nothing else. It was very small and had two dirty windows.

'We must be calm,' said Dimpi taking charge, 'We must not panic otherwise we will not be able to think. We must find a way to get out of here without the men's knowledge'.

'But how'? said Suman doubtfully. 'We are locked in and cannot possibly get out'.

Bunty peered through the windows in the gathering dusk and saw that there was an open field which was quite dry and treeless. Surprising since the rest of the district was very green.

They could hear the men talking among themselves in the next room. Suman went near the wall and began listening. Since she was from Bangalore she could understand Kannada, the language of Karnataka state, they were talking. Bunty and Dimpi couldn't understand a word as they were from Maharashtra and the language there was Marathi. They watched her changing expressions interestedly with some hope.

She put a finger to her lips and listened. A scared look came to her face and immediately Bunty and Dimpi hurried to her.

'What are they saying" they questioned but Suman was still listening.

After some time she turned to them and whispered, 'They are planning to take us to a place called Sivakasi in nearby Tamil Nadu state where they need children in the manufacturing unit of fireworks.'

'But why us?' wondered Dimpi aloud, 'There must be so many others ready to earn money for their families'.

'The Government has banned child labour,' explained Suman, 'Hence they cannot get local children. They need outsiders and kidnapping is their best bet. They may not harm us but they will make us work.'

'Then we can run away, 'said Bunty excitedly.

'Sometimes you can be really stupid,' said Suman scathingly, 'We will be like prisoners and they will keep a strict watch on us there. We won't be allowed to write or ring our people. I could understand all this from their talk. They know that you cannot understand Kannada hence they are not lowering their voices or keeping their plans a secret. They have reckoned without me knowing the language.' She explained.

'But where is Sivakasi?' asked Dimpi imagining a dingy room where all children were crowded together and made to work, a stern boss standing with a whip to see that they do. There were goose pimples on her back as she imagined being hit and kicked and shown no mercy.

'Somewhere in Tamilnadu, I think.' Said Suman a bit doubtfully. 'I read in the papers that children of Delhi had refused crackers and fireworks for the Diwali festival last year because each cracker had made some other child forget his childhood and work hard with no rest and no games or studies.'

Bunty and Dimpi felt sorry for those children and wondered whether they too would be producing fireworks for others.

It was now dark and there was no light in the room. Suman had gathered that they were to be kept prisoners for a day or two and then taken away. This was also to prevent any police search which they knew would be launched as soon as a complaint was filed. It was not easy to spirit away three children at a time.

'Fortunately we have some food and water,' said Bunty.

'How can you think of food at such a time?' wondered Dimpi aloud. 'I can think of nothing but Grandpa and Granny and how worried they must be. By now they may have even rung up our parents and informed them.'

Suddenly longing for Mummy and Daddy to be with them made them close to tears. The very thought of their dear parents and grandparents brought tears to the eyes of the three children who fell silent for some time. They had to escape from the clutches of the two horrible men but how?

Chapter 4

It was now nearing ten o'clock when Bunty suddenly said, 'I am hungry and am going to eat whatever we brought for our picnic. There is no point in wasting good food,' he continued on seeing Dimpi and Suman's worried faces, 'Things always have a way of looking better when there is food in the stomach. Besides,' he said warming up, 'These people have no intention of feeding us. They seem to be drinking, going by the clink of the glasses and loud guffaws.'

There was loud laughing and noisy shouting in the room adjoining them. There was no doubt that the two were in a relaxed mood, sure that the children were in a bolted room with no chance of getting out. It was also obvious that they had enough time on their hands.

Bunty now opened the lunch box and began eating. Slowly Dimpi and Suman also joined him and felt much better after eating. They had not realised how hungry they were. Never had bread and home made jam tasted better. Never had water tasted like nectar. They finished everything that Grandma had packed for them and then began thinking of ways of getting out. All three of them went round the small room to see if there was any weak wall in the dilapidated house. But they were not successful.

The bright rays of the full bright yellow moon guided them in their work. There were no trees to obscure the moon's rays and it was almost as if an electric light was shining in the room. They felt the windows carefully. The barred windows were too strong to break. The door too was sturdy despite being old and they could not hope to break it open as the men were just next door.

Suddenly Bunty looked up and seemed to get inspiration. He pulled the stool and stood on it. The sloping tiled ceiling was lower at the sides of the room and he could easily touch it. Inch by inch, foot by foot he searched the entire reachable space.

After about an hour's hard work, he grew excited.

Getting down from the stool he whispered, 'Suman, Dimpi, there is a loose tile here. We can remove it and climb out.'

'But' said Dimpi doubtfully, 'How can we remove it from inside? It will fall outside with a crash which will wake up these men. Also just one tile is too small.'

Bunty looked thoughtful. 'Yes,' he said at last, 'You are perfectly right. Let us put our heads together and think'.

Just then there was a sound outside of the bolt sliding open. The three children lay on the floor immediately and pretended to be asleep. From the corner of their eyes they could see the two men peering. Bunty thought of getting up and surprising them with a clout on the head but gave up the idea. They were too big and strong for him. Besides if they were not successful then every chance of escape would be closed.

'Fast asleep,' slurred the driver, 'We can also go back to sleep now.' This was said in Kannada which Suman told them later.

They waited for about half an hour and then got up. The children were sure that the men were fast asleep as there were no sounds except loud snores from them.

'See, Suman, I have been thinking,' said Bunty, 'You are the thinnest and the smallest and only you will be able to squeeze your way through the hole when we remove the tile.'

She looked doubtful and scared but knew that this was the only way.

'But Bunty, how can I remove the tile and not allow it to fall?' she questioned.

Bunty thought that over too.

'What you can do, Suman, is to climb on the stool and slowly remove the tile and then we can hoist you up and you can go out and open the door for us.' He said.

'You make it sound so easy,' she said, 'Okay, but it is difficult to hold the tile with one hand and also climb up.' She continued.

They pulled the bench just below the loose tile and slowly Bunty loosened it inch by inch till a small gap could be seen. The moon was still guiding them. He then told Dimpi to hold the tile while he pushed Suman through the small hole.

'Aren't we lucky that I am thin?' she whispered with a smile. Her heart was beating fast through fear and also excitement. They were having a real adventure and if they could be successful it would be so thrilling, they thought.

'Talk of luck only when we reach safely,' Dimpi, in return, whispered. They were straining and their hands were aching from the effort.

It took them a long time. Three people on a single bench standing almost on tiptoe, one holding the loosened tile, the other pushing the third above the hole. But eventually it was done and Suman jumped down from the roof with hardly any noise, thanks to her canvas shoes. She then carefully put the tile back in place.

The next step was to open the door of the room where Bunty and Dimpi were imprisoned. To do that Suman had to enter the house.

She went to the front door, only to be terribly disappointed. The door was firmly locked and nothing would open it.

She came to the window and whispered to them the bad news.

'There must be a back door, try that,' suggested Dimpi, 'Such houses always have more than one door.'

The back side of the house was in darkness and she had to wait till the moon came directly overhead for her to see. There were two doors but they too were locked securely to her disappointment and frustration. What was she to do?

Meanwhile Bunty and Dimpi were wondering what on earth Suman was doing and why she was taking such a long time. Suppose the men woke up and saw that there were only two children instead of three?

Dimpi began praying and kept her fingers crossed. Bunty tried to be brave though he too was getting more and more frightened.

Suman now began going round the house trying to find an open window or a door. After trying all the doors and the windows, she managed to find one that was slightly open. She slowly used force. The window was groaning a bit but Suman hoped that the men were fast asleep and that the window was on the other side of the dirty house.

When she got it reasonably wide open, she peeked inside. It seemed to be some sort of a storeroom as there were many things lying strewn about.

Besides, the window had no ledge and it was pretty difficult for her to climb inside.

Somehow she managed to get inside the dusty and the dirty room. She found herself in the pantry which led to a passage outside. Holding on to the walls she carefully moved.

Slowly picking her way she searched the house. She had been going around the house from outside so many times that she had lost her bearings. Besides it was quite dark inside the house where the moon's rays did not penetrate.

Something scampered and Suman nearly screamed. It was either a mouse or a lizard, she was not very sure but it was something that moved.

There seemed to be many rooms in the house and she wasted quite a lot of precious time trying to find out the room where the others were locked in.

On the third round of her search she was lucky. She found the room and slowly opened the door.

'Thank God, at last.' Said Dimpi.

'Whatever made you take so long?' questioned Bunty a trifle angrily.

'Now shut up and follow me,' she whispered.

Chapter 5

Hand in hand the three of them stepped out of the 'prison'. Trying to be very very quiet and on tiptoe they reached the door.

They opened the front door and were about to leave when Dimpi whispered, 'Wait' and rushed back.

She returned a minute later with a broad beaming smile on her face.

'What makes you smile?' asked Bunty curiously.

'I bolted their door from outside. They were snoring so loudly that they never even moved.'

'Oh, good, you really have some brains,' said Bunty admiringly, 'I would never have thought of it.'

They could see the taxi which had brought them here standing outside.

'If only we knew how to drive,' said Bunty, 'We would have been on the main road fast.' He went near the taxi and kicked it. 'This is the bad taxi that kidnapped us. I hate it.'

They found the rough lane and walked along it, the moon shining and guiding them all the way.

The three children walked fast as if the demons were behind them. Often they even broke into a run. The hooting of an owl made them jump in fear, so did the sudden braying of a donkey.

There appeared to be some dwelling houses nearby but they felt that they could not go and disturb people at this unearthly hour unless they really lost their way.

Actually there was no chance of losing their way as this was the only road available. And they had to just walk along it. It was barren and very dusty. After about half an hour they reached the main road and stood at the crossing wondering which way they should turn.

Right or left? They had no idea which way they had come or how far away they were from Chikmagalur. It was all so confusing.

A couple of vehicles passed by but they were afraid to ask for lifts, fearing another attempt at kidnapping. Now they were really very scared of all people and prayed that they would reach home safely and soon.

The eastern sky was turning pink and a cool breeze was making its presence felt when a police van passed by.

'Hey you,' shouted a policeman on seeing three bedraggled children sitting by the wayside, 'What are you doing here?'

'We are lost', said Suman in Kannada. She felt that the proper complaint should be lodged in a proper police station and it was not correct to give these policemen information which they may not use properly. He looked at them curiously and obviously wanted to ask more questions. However on seeing their tired and sleepy faces he changed his mind.

'Get in, I am taking you to the police station,' he said.

'Suman, what did he say?' questioned Bunty. Suman told him and they felt it was okay to get into the van as it was a police van and they climbed into the police van and sat down. Their tired feet needed rest and even though their eyes were closing they kept them open by talking to each other.

'He wanted to know about us but I told him that we were lost.' She replied.
'Why didn't you tell the truth?' asked Bunty curiously.

'I am not trusting anyone now,' Suman said, 'After the last one whom we trusted and who kidnapped us, I just can't take anyone at face value. How do we know that he is a real policeman? He may be dressed like one but he may be another thug.'

'What are you whispering' asked the policeman turning round and watching them curiously. 'How did you get lost in the first place? So far from Chikmagalur?'

'It just happened.' Answered Suman shortly refusing to divulge anything.

A little while later they were on the outskirts of Chikmagalur. The town was just waking up and the children remembered their Granny and her rangoli and milking of buffaloes early in the morning.

Today she and Grandpa must be very worried and may not have slept the whole night, they thought. Grandpa might really have had a heart attack on their not returning home yesterday and being out the whole night.

They reached the police station when they were on the point of nodding away. They had never seen it before and they looked around with great interest even though their eyes were almost closing. There was a lot of activity even though it was so early. Policemen were moving about going about their work.

The smart Thanedaar himself came to the door. He had seen them entering the police station from his window.

'Well, well, well, so the prodigals return.' He boomed as they got down from the van, 'Are you the Pai grandchildren?'

And when they nodded he said, 'You have created quite a sensation and your grandparents and half of Chikmagalur is very much worried. All are praying for you. What happened to you? Come and sit down. Tell me every detail of what happened and how you escaped from the clutches of those who kidnapped you.'

'Before that, Thanedaaar. Please allow us to ring our grandparents. They may not have slept the whole night and must be very worried.'

A phone was brought to them and they rang home. Grandpa picked it up at the very first ring, showing that he was near the phone every minute.

'Hello,', he said immediately, 'Any news of the children?'

'Grandpa, this is Bunty speaking,' said he. He could almost visualize the relief on Grandpa's face.

'Where are Dimpi and Suman? Are you alright? What happened? Where did you go? Where are you now?' questioned Grandpa the questions tumbling one after the other.

'We are all fin e, a lot dirty and dusty but otherwise okay. Don't worry, dear Grandpa. I will tell you all the details on coming home. Now we are at the Chikmagalur police station,' answered Bunty.

Grandpa suddenly put down the phone without any further talk and Bunty wondered whether Grandpa was so very angry that he did not even wait to say goodbye. He had wanted to speak but Grandpa had cut off.

The Thanedaar was waiting as the three children told the entire story in bits and pieces. He was very attentive scarcely saying a word but concentrating on their words. At some points he nodded. And he grew visibly excited when they described the two men. Two other senior policemen had now come to join the discussion and they exchanged glances when the children spoke about their kidnapping, shaking their heads over the description of the two men.

Before the story was completely told, in strode Grandpa and Grandma, her eyes red rimmed. They rushed and hugged the children as if never wanting to let them go.

'Oh, my darlings, oh darlings' said Grandma over and over again.

The story was told again to them and Suman piped in, 'Grandpa, because I knew Kannada I could know what was happening. And because I am so thin I could get out of the hole on the roof. I climbed through it and helped in the escape.'

'And Grandpa and Grandma it was my idea to lock the two scoundrels before coming here, otherwise they would have escaped by now.' Put in Dimpi proudly.

'And it was my idea to find the loose tile and push Suman out,' added Bunty, not to be left out.

'Oh dears you are all so smart and brave,' said Grandma wiping her eyes, 'But still you were kidnapped. Be very very careful in future.'

'Can we take then home now?' Asked Grandpa, 'They are tired, sleepy and dirty, they need to rest.'

'Yes, of course you can take them home. But they will have to come later to identify the criminals. They may have busted a gang of kidnappers which is operating in this region. The kidnapping was so very simple. And in broad daylight too. And three children. They must have thought that they got three children instead of one that they usually do.'

'Are the other kidnapped children found?' questioned Suman imagining a lot of kidnapped children pressed into hard work without the knowledge of their family. She could visualize the dark rooms, the hard work and the sad misery of all the children who were forced to work there.

'Now thanks to you we will begin our search and get these fellows to confess', said the big policeman gratefully. 'We cannot even explain how much we owe you, you have done our job.'

The three children with Grandpa and Grandma piled into the car and as they went home the three fell asleep in the car itself. Ramu had to literally pick them up, remove their shoes and socks and put them fully dressed into their beds. They were dead to the world and did not even know when Grandpa and Grandma peeped into their rooms at least a dozen times. There were so many visitors to their house as the news had spread fast and all were excited to hear the story from the children themselves. But Grandma was not allowing a single person to disturb them and they were left to sleep as long as they wanted.

When Bunty, Dimpi and Suman woke up it was bright daylight. It was two in the afternoon. They had slept for a full eight hours, dreaming of kidnappers and thieves. Suman even had a mouse running up her leg in her dream.

'We allowed you to sleep, patiently waiting for answers to our questions later on,' said Granny. 'I am going to perform an elaborate puja for your safe return.'

They had a sumptuous lunch and the three children ate as if they had not eaten for ages. Grandma had excelled herself in preparing all their favourite dishes and they did full justice to them. There were a lot of visitors who came to see the hero and heroines of the day. They had to answer so many questions till Grandma shooed all the people out.

Towards evening the local press interviewed them and right in the middle of the interviews and the photographs, a posse of policemen came. They were beaming and smiling.

They came to the children and presented them with large bouquets each. Red roses and white lilies were beautifully made into huge sweet smelling bouquets. 'From the police section for helping us solve the kidnapping case. In these last two months six children of this district have been kidnapped. We had never thought of Sivakasi. A delegation has gone there with the family members of the kidnapped children. If they are found you three will have earned enough 'punya' to last a lifetime'.

The Thanedaar also presented them a handsome cheque which they promptly donated to the local orphanage.

'So, Dimpi, I felt that this trip would be adventurous. Wasn't I right?' said Bunty having the last word as usual.

By Dr Veena Adige